The Widow's Noel

NIKKI ROBINSON

ILLUSTRATED BY JENNIFER KIRKHAM

This is a short story written in rhyme,
Of two lives coming to cross at Christmas time.

Our story is set on a snowy mountainside,

In an idyllic village less than one mile wide,

Hidden in a forest and surrounded by pine,

Is beautiful Auroratown – it's truly divine.

At the centre of town to join all people,

Is a medieval church with bells and steeple,

It embodies more than a choir and preacher,

Above the door is the following feature:

"Unity and togetherness is our belief,

We welcome all and grant relief,

So come on in and take joy in sharing,

Goodwill feelings of love, hope and caring."

Through the church window shines a dim hazy light,

It looks cosy and warm in the inky black night,

The choir is now singing for midnight mass,

Christmas Eve has already come to pass.

The Church it teems with Christmas mirth,

All in celebration of Jesus' birth,

The great tree stands at the centre of all,

Grand and mighty and impressively tall.

Nestled in its branches are candles aglow,

Sprinkled over them a dusting of snow,

Up atop the great tree – so far!

Twinkles a golden, glittering star.

Drifting through the sweet winter air,

Festive scents of cinnamon, orange and pear,

Beaming all around are townsfolk faces,

Upon which Christmas has etched magical traces.

Sitting outside is an abandoned hound,

Wistfully longing for what he hasn't yet found,

He hopes that as the service draws to a close,

Someone will take him in to settle his woes.

Still a stray – it remains a puzzle,

Small and cuddly with a shaggy brown muzzle,

Circling his right eye is a patch of white,

He really is a loveable sight.

Last Christmas as the morning broke,

In excitement two children awoke,

To their stockings they ran most quick,

Had he been, the jolly Saint Nick?

By the chimney the children froze,

Four paws there were and a snuffly nose,

Around his neck a red ribbon bow,

Their faces shone with a giddy glow.

He wagged his tail in frenzied joy,

And ran to them – the girl and boy,

They buried their faces in his shaggy fur,

Dearly he was loved at Christmas last year.

As the snow lay fresh on the ground,

Together the three could always be found,

Whether riding down hills in a sleigh,

Or huddled by the fire at the end of the day.

But as the snow began to thaw,

Time between cuddles grew much more,

Three player games dwindled in size,

Followed by head tilts and puppy dog eyes.

Instead of the New Year rekindling the spark,

Haunting the streets came a desperate bark,

One year on still alone in despair,

Craving simply an owner's collar to wear.

Yet our stray is not the only lone soul,

For whom a lack of company is taking its toll,

Inside the church on the backmost seat,

Sits an elderly woman struggling to stay upbeat.

Her husband she loved for fifty years plus one,

It feels so empty now that he's gone,

Her first Christmas without him by her side,

He'd been her companion, lover and guide.

This year's service is the very same,

As all those before it in tradition's name,

Everything down to the Christmas wreath,

All that's new is her heavy grief.

She closes her eyes and imagines him there,

Holding her hand with tender care,

She pictures his smile warm and wide,

How it wrinkled his eyes at the side.

Those honest eyes as brown as oak,

How he smelled of log fire and smoke,

His laugh so strong it shook his whole figure,

He went through life with the boldest vigour!

Christmas carols the choir are singing,

Each other's hands the townsfolk are wringing,

The Church bells – 12 o'clock they call,

"Merry Christmas! Merry Christmas! Goodwill tidings to all!"

Christmas Day is welcomed with cheer,

Into the night the townsfolk disappear,

Passing a stray on their way to retire,

They leave to hang stockings by the fire.

The widow inside chooses a candle to light,

For her husband it shines most bright,

As she stares deep into the flame,

She thinks of nothing but her late husband's name.

With a pitter and patter the silence does break,

A sniff and a snort jolt the widow awake,

Looking around for the cause of her fright,

The widow is moved by a heart-breaking sight.

A loveable stray with no owner to follow,

Is looking for shelter until the morrow,

Around his eye a mark whiter than snow,

He curls under the altar with nowhere to go.

She scoops him up in a warm embrace,

Holding him close as he licks her face,

Nuzzling her neck he wags his tail,

Down her cheek a tear makes its trail.

Some tinsel she takes from around the tree,

"Will you please come home with me?"

A collar of silver he wears with pride,

They leave the church side by side.

Together they make tracks in the snow,

With a woof and a bark he runs after a crow,

Up it soars with a squawk loud to hear,

She throws back her head to laugh bright and clear.

With a twinkle in her eye and a smile on her face,

She searches for something he can chase,

There on the frost lies a small oak stick,

After it he bounds – joyful and quick.

Upon reaching a door with homely charm,

She turns to him – loving and calm,

"Noel is now your very own name,

I knew someone once called just the same."

On their Christmas walks in the cold,

The townsfolk passed a snug abode,

Through the window many did peer,

Smiles they felt and heart-warming cheer.

Creating memories forever to share,

There inside an unusual pair,

A cracker they pulled with a noisy snap,

A widow knitting, companion on lap.

Unity and togetherness ended their grief,

Within each other they found relief,

The rest of their days they took joy in sharing,

Friendship founded in love, hope and caring.

Printed in Great Britain
by Amazon

33515655R00016